First published in Great Britain 2020 by Egmont UK Limited
2 Minster Court, 10th Floor, London EC3R 7BB

www.egmont.co.uk

Text copyright © Adam and Charlotte Guillain 2020
Illustrations copyright © Sam Lloyd 2020

The authors and illustrator have asserted their moral rights.

ISBN 978 1 4052 9418 8

A CIP catalogue record for this title is available from the British Library.

Stay safe online.
Egmont is not responsible for content hosted by third parties.

Egmont takes its responsibility to the planet and its inhabitants very seriously.
We aim to use papers from well-managed forests run by responsible suppliers.

ONE BANANA, TWO BANANAS

ADAM AND CHARLOTTE GUILLAIN
ILLUSTRATED BY SAM LLOYD

EGMONT

One banana, two bananas,

three bananas, **four,**

snoozing in the garden when . . .

DING-DONG!

Who's at the door?

Welcome to Banana Bungalow

Five bananas, **six** bananas, **seven** bananas . . .

...eight!
They're going to have a **party**
and they're going to stay up **late**.

Eight

bananas in pyjamas
bouncing on the beds.

"Upsydaisy!"

shout bananas, standing on their heads.

But **who** is at the window?
They just can't believe their eyes . . .

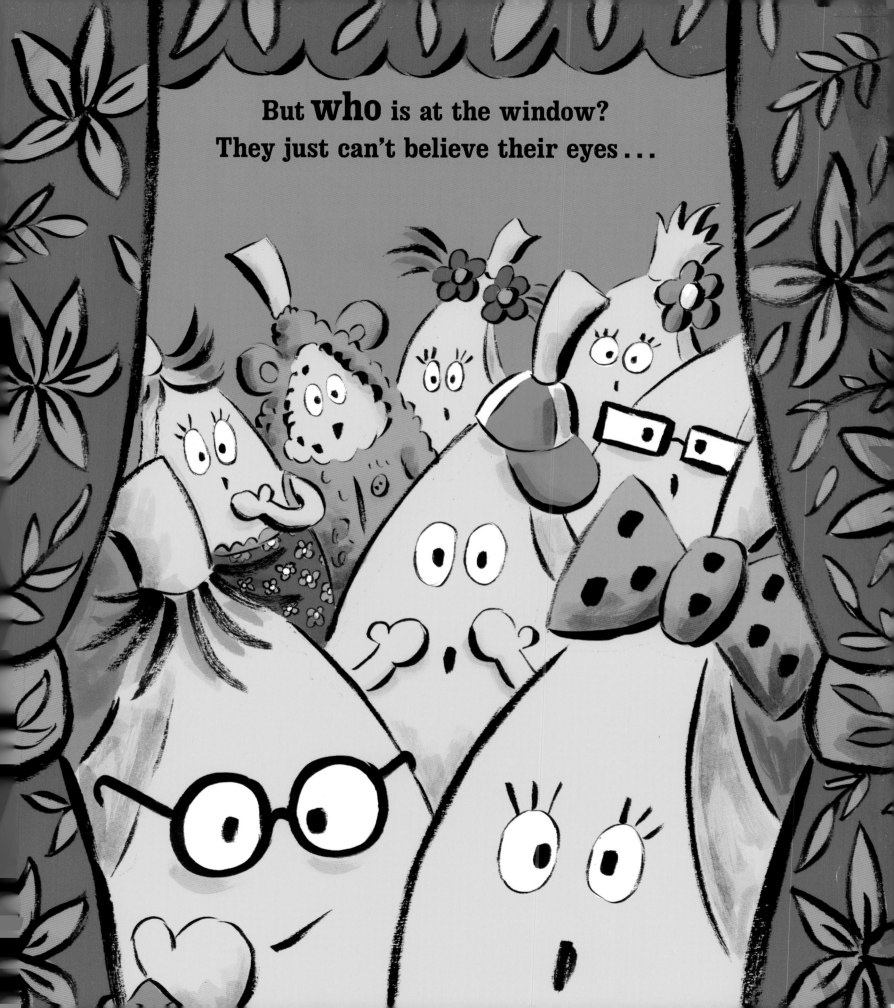

A llama panorama cries,

"We've got a **big surprise!**"

"We've come from
The Bahamas," says
one llama with a grin.

"We're going to have a llama race – you're welcome to join in."

Eight bananas in pyjamas in a llama race . . .

"Bananas!"
gasps a monkey and he quickly starts to chase.

Eight bananas leap off llamas –

Monkey licks his lips.

"Yikes!
What's that?" cries Monkey
as he stumbles and he slips!

A pair of super new bananas
come to make up **ten.**

Ten bananas shout at Monkey,

"Don't chase us again!"

But Monkey's feeling hungry and he doesn't care at all.
He scares the poor bananas as he leaps and makes them...

Splash

go **ten** bananas
as they topple in the lake.

"**Oh no!**" shout the bananas.
"This is such a **big** mistake!"

Ten bananas in pyjamas, swimming for their lives,
Chased by **ten** piranhas baring teeth as sharp as knives.

Oh! What's this? More trouble?
Monkey's jumped in a canoe!

Look out, **ten bananas!**
Monkey's coming after you!

Ten bananas panic – how much longer can they float?

But look – across the water speeds...

. . . a fast banana boat!

"We're sorry!" ten bananas cheer,
"We **will** not be your **lunch!**

And **you** can never catch us
as we're such
a clever bunch!"